# Parents and Caregivers,

Stone Arch Readers are designed to provide enjoyable reading experiences, as well as opportunities to develop vocabulary, literacy skills, and comprehension. Here are a few ways to support your beginning reader:

- Talk with your child about the ideas addressed in the story.

- Discuss each illustration, mentioning the characters, where they are, and what they are doing.

- Read with expression, pointing to each word. You may want to read the whole story through and then revisit parts of the story to ensure that the meanings of words or phrases are understood.

- Talk about why the character did what he or she did and what your child would do in that situation.

- Help your child connect with characters and events in the story.

Remember, reading with your child should be fun, not forced. Each moment spent reading with your child is a priceless investment in his or her literacy life.

Gail Saunders-Smith, Ph.D.

# STONE ARCH **READERS**

are published by Stone Arch Books
A Capstone Imprint
1710 Roe Crest Drive
North Mankato, Minnesota 56003
www.capstonepub.com

Library of Congress Cataloging-in-Publication Data
Suen, Anastasia.
The pirate map : a Robot and Rico story / by Anastasia Suen ; illustrated by Mike Laughead.
p. cm. — (Stone Arch readers)
ISBN 978-1-4342-1871-1 (library binding)
ISBN 978-1-4342-2301-2 (pbk.)
[1. Play—Fiction. 2. Pirates—Fiction. 3. Buried treasure—Fiction. 4. Robots—Fiction.]
I. Laughead, Mike, ill. II. Title.
PZ7.S94343Pi 2010
[E]—dc22
2009034208

Summary: Robot and Rico pretend to be pirates and look for buried treasure.

Art Director: Bob Lentz
Graphic Designer: Hilary Wacholz

Reading Consultants:
Gail Saunders-Smith, Ph.D.
Melinda Melton Crow, M.Ed.
Laurie K. Holland, Media Specialist

# The PIRATE MaP

A **ROBOT** **AND** **RiCO** STORY

BY ANASTASIA SUEN
ILLUSTRATED BY
MIKE LAUGHEAD

STONE ARCH BOOKS
a capstone imprint

This is ROBOT.
Robot has lots of tools.

He uses the tools to help his
best friend, **Rico**.

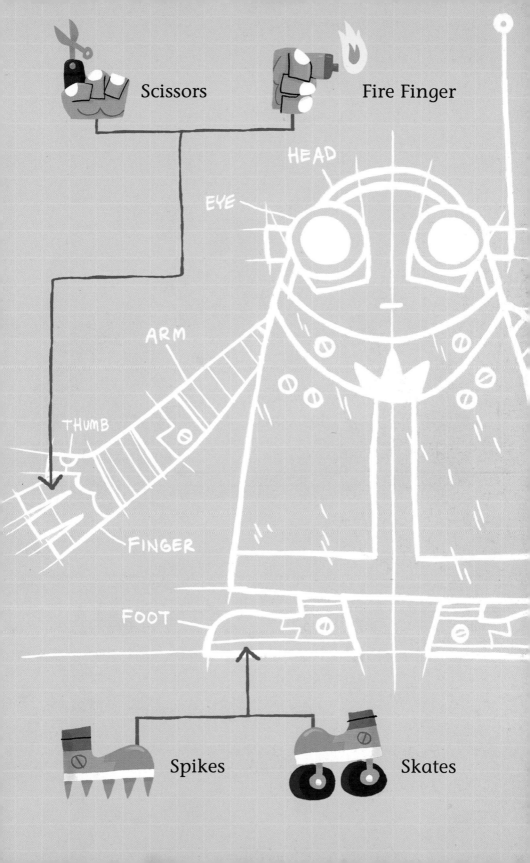

Scissors

Fire Finger

HEAD

EYE

ARM

THUMB

FINGER

FOOT

Spikes

Skates

Robot and Rico are very bored.

"Our TV show is over," says Robot.

"And the cookies are gone,"
says Rico.

"Now what?" says Rico.

"We can play pirates," says Robot.

"I have everything right here,"
says Robot.

"Cool! A pirate hat!" says Rico.

"I have swords and scarves,
too," says Robot.

"Fun! Let me try," says Rico.

"Now what?" asks Rico.

"I have one more thing,"
says Robot.

"Here it is," says Robot.

"What is it?" asks Rico.

"It's a map," says Robot.

"Is it a pirate map?" asks Rico.

"Maybe," says Robot. "X marks the spot."

"Let's go find that X," says Rico.

"Hurry!" says Rico.

"Not so fast," says Robot.

"We'll need these," says Robot.

"Which way?" asks Rico.

Robot looks at the map.

"That way," says Robot.

"Here we go," says Rico.

Robot and Rico walk up the
big hill.

Robot stops.

He looks at the map.

"Which way?" asks Rico.

"That way," says Robot.

Robot and Rico walk into the woods.

They walk and walk and walk.

"Let's rest by the river," says Rico.

"I'll check the map," says Robot. "The treasure must be close by."

Robot and Rico walk over to a
big rock.

"It must be here," says Robot.

"Let's start digging," says Rico.

"Look!" says Robot.

"What is in it?" asks Rico.

Robot slowly opens the box.

"Cookies!" says Rico.

"I like being a pirate," says Rico.

"I knew you would," says Robot.

# STORY WORDS

bored

cookies

pirates

swords

scarves

treasure

Total Word Count: 258

One robot. One boy. One crazy fun friendship! Read all the Robot and Rico adventures!